Today Is Halloween!

Written and illustrated by

P.K. Hallinan

For Tommy and Lisa

Ideals Children's Books • Nashville, Tennessee
an imprint of Hambleton-Hill Publishing, Inc.

Published by Ideals Children's Books
An imprint of Hambleton-Hill Publishing, Inc.
Nashville, Tennessee 37218

Printed and bound in the United States of America

ISBN 0-8249-8557-5

It's All Hallow's Eve!
Orange lamps glow like torches.
There are black cats in windows
and pumpkins on porches!

And just out your window,
the moon's growing bright.
It's time to get ready
for this wonderful night!

First, put on a costume—
whatever you choose—
a pirate in pigtails . . .
or a ghost in red shoes!

Now, pick out a bag—
a big one's just dandy.
But see that the handles
can handle the candy!

And the next thing you know,
you're ready to go!

Out on the street
where the dark shadows meet,
you see the first goblins
collecting their treats.

And up in the sky
where the clouds slither by,
you can almost see phantoms
beginning to fly.

And an icy wind moans
like the rattling of bones . . .

Ah, but here come some friends
from out of the dark—
why it's Freddy the Wolfman
and Dracula Clark!

Here comes Calamity Sue
on her horse,
accompanied by Sally—
an angel, of course.

And with Rock 'n' Roll Pete,
your group is complete.

There's a horrible howling,
then a terrible roar!
You move as one bunch
to the very first door.

The lights start to flicker!
Someone's flipping a switch!
The creaky door opens . . .
Oh no, it's a witch!

"Trick or treat!" you say weakly,
then meekly stand back.
But the witch cackles kindly,
with gifts for each sack.

And with candy in tow,
off you all go.

At the next house a spider
is offering cider.

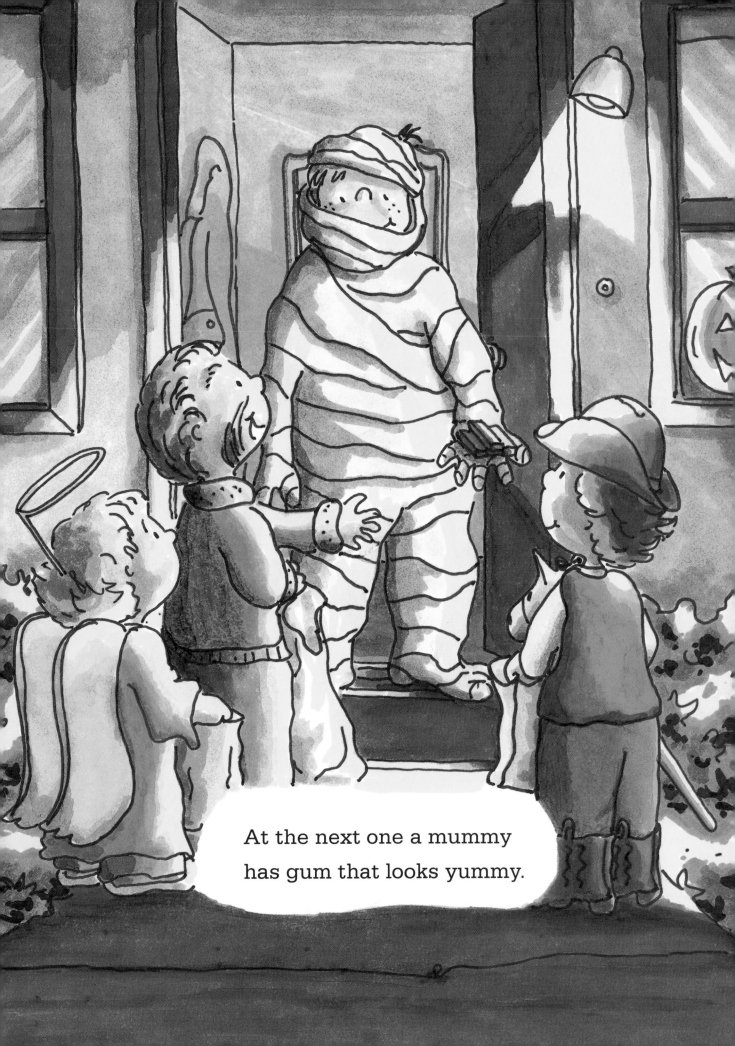

At the next one a mummy
has gum that looks yummy.

Each house is so different,
some scary, some cute.
But you always say "thank you"
—even for fruit.

Alas, it must end,
the haunting, the fun,
for the bag that you're dragging
now weighs half a ton.

So you slowly head home
as you watch a bat zoom
like a mad flying ace
'cross the face of the moon.

At home you sit down
to carefully pour
the goodies you've gotten
all over the floor.

And everything's special,
so Mom helps you sift
the candy from the apples,
the gum from the gifts.

What a great bunch of goodies!
What a nice pile of treats!
You'd like to start snacking,
but it's too late to eat.

So you lay back your head,
and sigh as you say . . .

"I love Halloween!
What a wonderful day!"